HUMANO MORPHS

AIR MORPH ONE: READY FOR TAKEOFF

M. D. Spenser

Paradise Press, Inc.

Weston, FL

32124-4

9 200

Our Price

Published by Paradise Press, Inc. by arrangement with River Publishing, Inc. All right, title and interest to the "HUMANOMORPHS" logo and design are owned by River Publishing, Inc. No portion of the "HUMANOMORPHS" logo and design may be reproduced in part or whole without prior written permission from River Publishing, Inc. An application for a registered trademark of the "HUMANO-MORPHS" logo and design is pending with the Federal Patent and Trademark office.

ISBN 1-57657-334-6

EXCLUSIVE DISTRIBUTION BY PARADISE PRESS, INC.

Cover Design & Illustrations by Nicholas Forder

Printed in the U.S.A.

For Barb, again, with love.

Chapter One

I gazed longingly at my poster of Mount Rushmore, sighed, grabbed my book bag, and headed out the door, moaning all the way.

My seventh grade class was going on a science field trip.

I love Mount Rushmore. I hate science. Science, if you want my opinion, really stinks. Big time. Plus, it's like really, really boring.

Mount Rushmore, in case you didn't know, is a mountain in the Black Hills of South Dakota. The heads of four U.S. presidents have been carved right into the cliff. Each head is sixty feet high, or about as tall as ten of my dads would be if each one were standing on the head of the dad below.

In other words, they're huge.

I know, because I've seen them in person. I bugged my parents so much they finally took me. Six times.

And why not? South Dakota is the next state

north of Nebraska, so it's not that far. It's not as if I was bugging them to take me to Disney World or some other place in Florida.

Florida is about a zillion miles from Nebraska. It's so far that, if you drove, you could start the trip when you were a kid and not wind up getting there until you were a teenager. Or maybe even an adult.

Your parents would be positively ancient.

Besides, I don't want to go to Disney World. I know, I know — I'm a little unusual. "Quite odd, actually," is how my friend Freddy puts it.

But then Freddy is a little unusual himself. He likes science, for one thing.

Anyway, as I was saying, I love Mount Rushmore. The presidents carved into the mountainside are George Washington, Thomas Jefferson, Abraham Lincoln and Theodore Roosevelt.

I hope that one day they'll make room for one more.

Me.

Because I'm going to be president sooner or later. Presidents don't need to know science.

We've had generals as presidents, and lawyers and farmers and even a movie actor. You know how many biologists have been president? None. Zee-ro.

I glanced once more at my poster of Mount

Rushmore, with the great stone presidential heads lit with the rosy glow of sunset, sighed again and headed out to meet my fate — a dumb old science field trip.

I didn't realize it then — I had no way of knowing — but this field trip would change my life, and come pretty darn close to ending it.

Chapter Two

There are some things you should know before you read any more of my story.

First of all, it's true. Every word. Believe me, there is no way I could make something like this up. They say that truth is stranger than fiction, and now I know they're right.

Second, I suppose I ought to introduce myself. My name is Melvin.

I'm not going to tell you my last name, because then some people would read this book and make fun of me. They wouldn't believe that this all really happened, and they'd call me a nut.

No one needs that. At least I don't.

It's like when people see UFOs and then tell the authorities. Everybody calls them crazy.

Just imagine that you had seen a flying saucer glowing in the night sky as plain as the moon, and you knew for a fact that you had seen it and that you weren't crazy. Then when you walked down the street, people rolled their eyes and pointed at their heads and made circling motions.

Well, this story is a lot stranger than if I had just seen a plain old ordinary flying saucer. And I just don't need that kind of abuse.

Atkinson, Nebraska, is a small town. It's not like a big city, like Detroit or Los Angeles, where you can lose yourself in a crowd. You could take the entire population of Atkinson and you wouldn't even fill a football stadium.

Heck, you would barely even fill a barbershop.

So if I said something that sounded crazy, even though it was really the truth, everyone in town would make fun of me. There would be no escaping it. I couldn't move to a new block or go to a new school and start fresh.

Still, what happened to me is important. People need to know about it. That's why I'm writing this down but leaving out my last name. Atkinson, Nebraska, is a small town, but about twenty people here are named Melvin. It may be the most popular first name in town.

Atkinson sits on the banks of the Elkhorn River. Actually, when it floods, Atkinson sits under the surface of the Elkhorn River, which is darned inconvenient. All of us have to leave our homes and

5

sleep on the floor of the high school gymnasium.

That has only happened once since I've been alive. But the old-timers who gather at Melvin's Barbershop on Main Street (I told you there are a lot of people here named Melvin) always talk about all the times Atkinson has flooded in the past. They like to point to stains on the sides of buildings and tell you that this is how high the water rose in 1927.

That was the year the Mississippi River had a terrible flood that forced a million people out of their homes. You couldn't fit that many people in our high school gymnasium, I can tell you that.

The way I understand it, the waters of the Mississippi River that year backed up into the Missouri River. Then the waters of the Missouri backed up into the Platte River, and the waters of the Platte backed up into the Elkhorn River, and the waters of the Elkhorn backed up into Melvin's Barbershop.

A guy named Herbert Hoover handled the emergency for the federal government, and he did such a good job of it that he got elected president the very next year.

I know a lot about the presidents.

The year it flooded when I was alive, I remember a lot of dogs stuck on the roofs of houses, howling their heads off. They were scared and it was sad.

I would have liked to have handled the flood

6

emergency that year so I could have gotten elected president the next year, but I was too young to handle the emergency — and too young to be president, too.

You have to be thirty-five to get elected president.

I think that takes away from the democratic rights of voters. If everybody in the country wants to vote for a twelve-year-old kid for president, they ought to be able to. That's their choice. They're allowed to vote for total idiots, aren't they?

To rule kids out is discrimination, in my opinion.

This particular day, though, my views on the Constitution of the United States were not particularly relevant. I had a science field trip to take. While I know a lot about the presidents, I know darn little about science.

The only thing I know about it is that, judging from the kids who are good at it, studying science must give you zits. Lots of them.

Chapter Three

The white cement walls of the Nacirema Dairy Production and Research Center loomed before us.

Mrs. Ziggernaut, our seventh grade science teacher whom everyone called Mrs. Ziggersnot, had brought us to see a cow milking factory.

Oh, joy.

Everyone in Atkinson has seen a cow milked. Actually, everyone in Atkinson has probably milked a cow personally, now that I think about it.

But Mrs. Ziggersnot said this brand new dairy factory was a state-of-the-art place, using the latest scientific methods, and it was worth seeing.

"OK, now we've seen it," I muttered to my friend Freddy as we piled out of the school bus. "Can we leave now?"

"Come on, Melvin," Freddy said. "This is going to be really neat — to anyone with an open mind, that is."

I gave him a punch in the shoulder. Freddy was

my best friend, even if he did like science.

He and I had known each other since first grade. People say we usually choose friends who are similar to us. You know, birds of a feather flock together.

Well, that wasn't true of Freddy and me. We were different in lots of ways. I was always trying — and failing — to convince him that the presidents were very interesting.

He was always trying — and failing — to convince me that science is simply fascinating.

I was kind of an extrovert. I talked and joked a lot. I liked to be the center of attention.

Freddy was kind of an introvert. He didn't say much, and he didn't joke that much either, though he kidded around with me sometimes. He rarely took center stage, preferring to observe things quietly from the sidelines.

I'm white. I have blond hair, with a cowlick that sticks up on the back of my head, and I get freckles in the summer.

Freddy is an Omaha Indian. He has dark skin, piercing brown eyes, and black hair done into a long braid. He was also one of the rare exceptions to the science-gives-you-zits rule.

But I suppose we had some similarities, even if

they weren't apparent on the surface.

We were both pretty bright. I did well in social studies and English, and coasted along in my other classes. Freddy did well in science and math, and coasted along in the rest.

The main thing, I think, is that we were both honest. With Freddy, you always knew where you stood. I liked that. He always knew where I stood, too. Neither one of us played games, like being nice to people we were really angry with, or anything like that.

And we were both pretty forgiving. We'd get mad at each other, but we'd get over it. When the argument was done, it was over for good. Neither one of us held grudges.

"Yeah, right," I said to him as we stood by the bus. "This will be really neat. A scientific milking factory."

He gave me a shove, and I pretended I was going to punch him again.

"Boys! Boys!" Mrs. Ziggersnot called out, which I thought was kind of a ridiculous thing to say. I felt like replying, "Yes, indeed we are, Mrs. Ziggernaut! How did you ever guess?"

But I kept quiet, which was probably a good thing for me.

Mrs. Ziggersnot kept trying to get us to line up two-by-two, like little soldiers on parade. We kept ignoring her. Finally she gave up and led us up to the double glass doors of the huge cement building.

The doors were locked, bolted fast.

Chapter Four

The Nacirema Dairy Production and Research Center stood white and massive right on the banks of the Elkhorn River. Sun glinted off the surface of the water as it flowed behind the factory, winking and twinkling in the reflected blue of the sky.

Wide fields spread on either side of the dairy center. I supposed that was where the cows grazed when they weren't inside getting scientifically milked.

The whole area was surrounded by a huge wire fence. Our bus driver had been required to show a special pass when we entered the gate.

I remembered when construction workers had swarmed into the area to build the factory. I went down to try to get a look a couple of times, but they wouldn't allow anyone near. I guess it was a safety regulation; maybe they were afraid of getting sued if someone got hurt and wasn't wearing a hard-hat.

It surprised me that they were building the place so close to the river. I figured that was because they were all from out of town. They hadn't heard the stories the old-timers tell at Melvin's Barbershop, or seen them point to the old water marks from the floods of long ago.

But, I thought, hey, if the place floods — or, I should say, *when* the place floods — they'll find out soon enough. There will be a lot of panicked cows, I thought, though I couldn't imagine cows managing to climb onto the roof the way all the dogs had.

Some kids ahead of me were yanking on the doors. "Hey, Mrs. Ziggernaut, it's locked!" they shouted. No one called her Mrs. Ziggersnot to her face.

"Can we leave now?" I muttered to Freddy.

He just looked at me and rolled his eyes.

It turned out that Mrs. Ziggersnot had known the doors would be locked. She walked to the front of the line, said "Boys! Boys! Stop pulling!" and pressed a button beside the doors.

A tinny-sounding voice blared though a speaker. "Identify yourself, please," it said.

"Um-hmmm-hmmh," Mrs. Ziggernaut said, clearing her throat importantly. She adjusted her spectacles and felt to see that her hair bun was neatly in place, as she always did on official occasions. "This is Mrs. Clara M. Ziggernaut with her seventh-grade

13

science class from Elkhorn Middle School. We have, um-hmmm-hmmh, an appointment."

The doors buzzed electronically, and I heard the click of the lock opening. Mrs. Ziggernaut pulled one of the doors open and we filed in.

The first thing I noticed was how incredibly thick the walls of this place were. I looked as I passed through the doors, and I was astonished. They had to be three feet thick. Were they afraid the cows were going to stage a breakout?

The next thing I noticed was how clean and white and sterile this place looked. I had expected something a little more barn-like, with a hint of cow dung on the floor and a hint of cow stink in the air.

The only thing I smelled was disinfectant.

We stood in the lobby, which was deserted. I saw no people, no desks, no reception area, no pictures on the wall.

Soon, however, I heard a clicking coming down a hallway. A woman in a white blouse and a tight black skirt emerged. She wore quite a bit of make-up and her lipstick was very red. The clicking was from her high heels; her skirt was so tight she could only take little bitty baby steps.

"Welcome," she said, and she smiled without looking happy. "We're delighted you came to tour the

Nacirema Dairy Production and Research Center today. We trust your tour will be both informative and pleasant."

She spoke every word in the same tone. Her voice didn't rise and fall the way normal people's voices do.

Freddy looked at me, leaned close to my ear, and whispered, "Is this woman a robot or what?"

"No," I whispered back. "Just a former flight attendant."

Our guide announced that her name was Jane Smith, and that we were to follow her, and that on no account were we to get separated from her and go off exploring on our own.

Then she whirled around and clicked off down the long white hallway. We tromped along behind.

Soon we reached a closed set of double doors. On one side, I noticed a round hole in the wall that was filled with a reddish glow.

"This is Checkpoint One," said Jane Smith. "Before proceeding further, all of you will have your fingerprints electronically scanned and digitally recorded."

Chapter Five

Freddy wrinkled his forehead. He always does that when he's thinking really hard.

"This makes no sense," he said. "Absolutely no sense at all."

"That's science for you," I replied cheerfully. "None of it makes any sense."

One by one, each of us stepped up and put his hand in the hole in the wall. When it was my turn, my entire hand was bathed with the red glow. After about two seconds, a voice came out of the wall saying, "Please state name and address."

I did that and two seconds later the voice announced, "Prints recorded." It was time for the next person to take his turn.

Freddy was still wrinkling his forehead. His deep brown eyes looked troubled. He really likes to understand things, and it bothers him a lot when he can't figure things out.

Finally he raised his hand. "Miss Smith?" he

asked.

She looked at him and raised her eyebrows.

"I was just wondering ma'am," he said. "Why do you have such heavy security at a dairy plant?"

Miss Smith stared at Freddy for about five seconds, as if she were trying to bore a hole in his forehead with her eyes.

Finally she said, "Perhaps you have heard of mad cow disease. It ravaged dairy herds in Europe, particularly in the British Isles. Thousands of cows had to be destroyed to prevent the disease from spreading further."

Freddy nodded. "I read about it," he said. "It can be spread from cows to humans, and it causes a deadly brain disease in people."

"That is correct," Miss Smith said. "And not only can the disease be spread from cows to humans, it can also be spread from humans to cows. If any cows in this facility should happen to come down with mad cow disease, we will be able to track down the source. We will have a computerized record of the name, address and fingerprints of every person who has ever visited."

She paused, and a smug little smile crossed her lips.

"That is just one of the many scientific innovations at this fine facility," she said. "Now, if you'll just follow me . . ."

Chapter Six

When I think back on that fateful visit to the Nacirema Dairy Production and Research Center, three things stand out in my mind above all others.

One is the absence of people. The second is the incredible sound in the milking center. And the third is what I saw out the window of the milking center, a sight I will never forget.

It amazed me to realize that almost no human beings worked there. When we passed through the doors after being fingerprinted, I did see a couple of people in a glass booth full of control panels and lights and knobs and switches. It looked like an air traffic control tower.

Miss Smith explained that the people in the glass booth controlled the doors, and the flow of milk from the cows to the pasteurization center and from there to the homogenization chamber.

They controlled the temperature of the milk — normally quite cold, but hot when it was being pasteurized to kill bacteria — to within a tenth of a degree Fahrenheit. They controlled the amount of food each cow received each day to within a tenth of an ounce.

I did see a couple of other people down a hallway wearing bulky white space suits. Miss Smith explained that it was important to keep the milk in a completely sterile environment after it was pasteurized. Any bacteria, she said, would lead to fermentation — in other words, the milk would go sour before it reached the stores.

When we reached the doors leading into the milking center, Miss Smith spoke into an intercom, and one of the people in the glass booth pressed a button.

Each cow had her neck clamped in place. Food dropped from a chute in front of each cow's face. A clean cement trench ran behind each row of cows, catching, shall we say, the droppings, which were then washed away by an automatic system of high-pressure hoses.

Wow, I thought. This sure beats the system at my uncle Melvin's farm, where you have to personally shovel the cow doody into a cart, wheel it outside and spread it on the fields.

That takes a lot of shoveling, and I can tell you from first-hand experience that cow doody is extremely heavy stuff.

And the sound — how can I describe it?

You know the slurping sound you make when you're trying to suck the last bit of milkshake through your straw from the very bottom of your cup?

It drives my mom crazy when I make that sound. Whenever she's around I make the sound a little louder just to see if I can annoy her.

Well, to understand the sound in the milking center, you have to start with one kid's milkshake slurp and then multiply it. By a lot.

The cows were hooked up to milking machines, which sucked the milk out of their udders and through stainless steel pipes off to storage containers and the pasteurization center, and so forth.

Two thousand cows stood lined up in that giant hall.

So that meant the noise in the milking center sounded like eight thousand kids standing side by side, all simultaneously trying to slurp the last few drops of milkshakes through their eight thousand straws in a pulsating rhythm.

That's a lot of slurping.

Miss Smith was talking quite loudly, trying to make herself heard over the roar of the slurps. She started explaining how the diet of each cow was scientifically designed to make that specific cow produce the most milk.

Then she went into food analysis. She discussed complex carbohydrates and the difference between different kinds of sugars, like glucose and dextrose and fructose. She described the proteins contained in gluten, and the peculiarities of the digestive systems of cows.

I tried to pay attention. I knew Freddy would want to discuss all this fascinating information when we got out of there, and I liked it when he paid attention to the stuff that interests me.

But it was no use. My mind wandered. I looked at the ceiling. I checked for dirt under my fingernails. I gazed out the window at the fields beyond.

That was when I saw it.

In the middle of one of the fields, I spotted a small lagoon. The water looked clear enough. I saw reflected in the surface the blue of the sky and some dark clouds moving in from the west.

That's funny, I thought. The weather was clear as a bell when we arrived.

Then, on the far bank of the lagoon, I noticed a large black form. It lay there motionless.

I squinted, trying to adjust my eyes to the light. The form had prongs of a sort stuck out stiffly from it.

I realized then that it was a cow, lying on its

side with its legs splayed. The cow, obviously, was quite dead.

I started to point out the window. My lips moved to ask a question, but no sound came.

Then, as I stared out the window, a meadowlark landed in the grass a few feet from the lagoon. The little bird turned its head this way and that, hopped toward the lagoon, and strutted proudly along the water's edge.

Then it turned its head both ways, leaned forward and dipped its beak in the water to drink. Then it opened its beak and seemed to choke. It tried to fly, but could not. Instead, it staggered around in a circle — then fell over stone dead under the darkening sky.

Chapter Seven

Freddy could not believe what I was telling him.

I had been so shocked by what I had seen through the window that I had said nothing about it at the time, and I had asked no questions.

I remembered how hard Miss Smith had stared at Freddy when he had asked what seemed like a reasonable question. Something inside me said it would be better if Miss Smith didn't even know what I had seen. So I didn't ask her.

I plodded through the rest of the tour in a daze, wondering why there might be a pool of poison water in the field outside the milk plant.

By the time we left, with Miss Smith waving at us and smiling without looking happy, the dark clouds had covered the sky completely. It wasn't raining hard, just spitting a bit. Little raindrops pelted us as we headed for the bus.

Now Freddy and I sat in my room under the

gaze of various presidents, discussing what I had seen. I had Mount Rushmore tacked on one wall. And I had posters of Washington, Lincoln, and John F. Kennedy taped to the other three walls.

"None of it makes any sense," Freddy said. "None of it — not the heavy security, not the people in space suits, and least of all the poisonous lagoon in the field."

"And you know what else?" I said. "I looked at the walls of that place as we walked in the front door, and they had to be three feet thick. Who ever heard of a dairy barn with walls like that? It's like a bomb shelter, for Pete's sake! I'll tell you what I think — scientists sure have a weird way of making milk."

We argued back and forth a little after that.

Freddy said we had to find a way to figure out what was really going on at the factory. I said that was impossible, because no one could possibly understand science, probably not even the scientists themselves.

Freddy was quiet and insistent. I was loud and skeptical.

I suggested a game of checkers. Freddy said we had to find out.

I suggested listening to some music. Freddy said we had to find out.

I suggested going downstairs for a snack.

Freddy said we had to find out.

Finally, I exploded.

"Why?" I demanded. "I don't *care* what's going on at that state-of-the-art milk factory? *Why* do we have to find out?"

"Because," Freddy said very quietly, "it might be dangerous."

"All the more reason to stay away!" I shouted in exasperation.

"All the more reason to find out," Freddy said calmly. I hate it when he stays calm when we're arguing.

"Well, how?" I asked. "How are two twelve-year-old kids going to find out what's going on out there, as you put it?"

"There's only one way," Freddy said. "And that's the scientific method. Look, that factory is in the flood plain. If some part of their process is producing poison, and the waters rise — as one day they will — it could pollute the river. Fish could die, and maybe even the raccoons and deer and bear that drink from the river."

He smiled a wry smile.

"And the river belongs to all of us," he added. "Particularly, if I may say so, Native Americans like me."

I sighed. He had me there.

"Fine," I said. "And just what *is* the scientific method in this case?"

"There's only one thing to do," Freddy said. "We have to get a sample of that water so we can have it analyzed."

Chapter Eight

It was pitch black and raining hard as we approached the fence that surrounded the Nacirema Dairy Production and Research Center.

My hair was matted to my scalp. Rain dripped off my nose. My clothes were soaked clean through and they stuck to my skin like mud. I shivered.

I could not believe Freddy had talked me into this.

"C'mon, Freddy," I pleaded. "Look, there's no way in. Let's go home."

I might as well have been talking to a deaf person. Freddy made no response at all. He just continued as if he hadn't heard a word I had said.

It was after midnight. I knew that because our plan had been to meet in front of my house right at midnight, and then walk down to the milk plant together. I had fallen blissfully asleep, hoping that Freddy, who never really joked, had suddenly begun and was kidding about going on this little adventure.

I was still blissfully asleep at midnight, dreaming that I was the president of the United States and was negotiating with the president of Russia. I was so successful that we banned all nuclear weapons from the face of the earth forever.

Freddy, who had *not* suddenly begun joking for the first time in his life, had to throw pebbles at my window to wake me up.

Now here we were in the dark, soaked to the skin, creeping slowly along the fence outside the milk factory. We were looking, if you can believe it, for a place where the dirt was soft enough for us to dig a little tunnel under the fence.

Freddy had explained — and I had agreed — that if security *inside* the dairy building was so tight, surely the fence was wired to an alarm. Any attempt to slice through the fence with wire cutters would trigger the alarm. And probably any attempt to climb over the fence would trigger the alarm, too.

I could picture searchlights and sirens suddenly going off, and the police coming, and me riding off in the back of a police car. I'd be delivered home, a policeman dragging me firmly by the ear, to find myself saying, "Well, you see, Mom, it's like this . . . "

Only then, I was quite sure, no words would come.

I felt like whining at Freddy one more time,

but I knew it would do no good. Besides, I thought, if I was going to be president one day, I was going to have to learn to show a little leadership.

I probed the ground along the fence, looking for a soft spot.

"Here," I whispered in a firm, leader-like kind of way. "Freddy. Psst. This is our spot."

Freddy came over and probed the area with the shovel he had carried under his arm.

"Good one, Melvin," he said. "I think this will do."

Before we started digging, Freddy said an Omaha prayer. It would not guarantee success, he said, but it always helped to have the spirits on your side, or at least to let them know you were thinking about them.

I could barely see him in the darkness. But I saw that he spread his arms wide and lifted his face to the rain as he chanted. I didn't catch the words, but somehow they comforted me.

We took turns with the shovel. It was hard work, even though the ground was soft. The rain had made the dirt heavy, and shoveling a big enough hole to allow us to crawl under the fence took a lot of time.

Plus, we had to be careful not to bump the shovel into the fence itself, in case it was equipped with motion sensors. And we couldn't just fling the dirt over our shoulders, either.

At my insistence, we piled it in one spot so that we could fill in the hole after we were done. I hoped no one would notice that anyone had entered the compound. The last thing I wanted was some big investigation.

That was one thing I had learned from studying presidents and their political techniques: Always cover your tracks.

I don't know how you can tell if you're sweating in the rain, but I sure felt like I was. My hands were sore and my back was stiff.

Finally, the hole seemed big enough for us to try to wriggle through.

My heart was pounding in my chest and I could barely breathe, but I went first. I had not thought up this whole plan, but future presidents do not just tag along. They lead the way.

I didn't want to dive face down in the mud, so I slid under the fence on my back. And a muddy experience it was.

Pushing with my feet, I slid through the ooze. I held my breath and sucked in my stomach, not wanting to bump into the fence. Then I climbed out of the hole on the other side.

Freddy shoved through the tote bag with our gear. I grabbed it. Then he slid through on his belly and emerged, muddy and smiling, beside me.

I waited for lights to flash on and alarms to sound and guards to come running.

But nothing happened. No light cut the darkness. I heard no noise but that of the raindrops slapping the grass. Nothing moved.

We were alone. And we were inside the compound.

Chapter Nine

Freddy opened the tote bag, took out a flash-light and turned it on.

"No!" I whispered in a firm, leader-like way. "If we use the flashlight, someone will spot us."

"If we don't use the flashlight, we might stumble straight into that poisonous lagoon and wind up dead, just like that little bird you saw," Freddy replied.

"Right," I said. "Let's use the flashlight." An effective leader always listens to good advice.

I took the light and led the way. After all, Freddy had not seen the lagoon, having been too interested in the science of milking to look out the window. He had no way of knowing where, exactly, the lagoon was.

We crept carefully across the field, walking in the general direction I thought would lead us to the water.

It's funny to think about it, looking back, but we both walked hunched over. There was no reason to do that: If someone spotted the flashlight beam waving around out in the field, well, then they had spotted us, whether we were hunched over or walking tall.

I guess walking bent over just made us *feel* more stealthy.

All of a sudden, I jumped.

I saw another flashlight beam waving around out in the field! Someone else was there!

Quickly, I turned my flashlight off. I turned around and motioned to Freddy to hold still. But he couldn't see me because, with the light off, it was pitch dark. In a second, he bumped into me.

"Shhhh!" I whispered. "I think someone else is out here."

With my heart pounding in my throat, I turned to the front again. I could feel Freddy holding tightly to my arm. I don't think either of us breathed.

I couldn't see the other flashlight. I looked all around, straining my eyes in the darkness. I saw nothing.

Whoever else was out there had turned his flashlight off, too.

I thought that maybe this was some kind of deadly game, one in which he was the hunter and we were the prey — only in this game, neither of us could see the other.

Or perhaps whoever else was out in the field was just trying to spook us. If so, he was doing a pretty good job.

I held my breath, kept every muscle taut and still, and listened with all my might.

I heard the patter of rain on the ground. I heard crickets humming in the grass. I heard the running of the Elkhorn River behind the factory. In the distance, back in town, a car rumbled along a road to somewhere else.

I listened for a long minute, but I heard nothing else.

Then, suddenly, I understood.

I drew a deep breath and tried to settle down. Still my heart pounded wildly. I breathed in and out, deeply, and tried to relax all my muscles.

There was no one else in the field. There never had been.

What I had seen was the reflection of my own flashlight beam, sweeping back and forth across the lagoon.

The lagoon!

"We found it!" I exclaimed, loud enough to make Freddy jump. The rain was dripping off my face and I could feel myself smiling in the dark.

"Sheesh," Freddy said. "First you need everything quiet as a mouse, and then you start yelling out across the field. Make up your mind, will you?"

"Sorry," I said.

I flicked the flashlight on again. We crept forward again, staring at the wet blades of grass gleaming in the beam of light. We didn't want to rush forward without thinking and blunder right into the lagoon.

Then we saw the reflection again, the beam of my light playing across the surface of the water.

I shone the light a little closer. We saw where the grass ended. The lagoon was surrounded by a wide swath of brown dirt where nothing grew.

Three more steps and we were there.

"OK, Freddy," I said. "What now?"

Chapter Ten

"Shine the light all the way around the edge of the water," Freddy said. "I want to get a look at this dead cow."

Slowly, I directed the flashlight beam around the entire shore of the lagoon.

There was no dead cow. Nor was there any sign of a dead bird.

They were gone.

But I knew that I had seen them.

"Really, Freddy, I . . . "

He held out his hand to stop me. I did not need to explain further, at least not to him. He believed me without question.

"They *know*," he said softly. "They've removed the carcasses, the dead bodies. That means they *know* the lagoon is poisonous."

He set the tote bag on the ground and unzipped it.

"Stay back from the water," he said. "If it

37

killed the bird that fast, believe me, we don't want any contact with it."

"Right," I said. "Good advice. I'd just as soon not keel over dead right here tonight. I kind of had in mind living another sixty or seventy years. Or long enough anyway to get elected president."

Freddy made no reply. He was, in general, a quieter person than I was. And he had long since grown used to my constant talk about becoming president.

One reason I liked him, actually, was that he never made fun of my ambition. The other kids did. They rolled their eyes and laughed. But Freddy only said that you never know what you can achieve until you try.

We all have the power to change ourselves into whatever we want to be, he said. It's not easy, he said. It takes work. It takes honesty. But he kept saying that, if we're willing to try, we can make ourselves better people — kinder, more loving, more in tune with nature.

If your motives are pure and you want to accomplish something good rather than just getting famous and powerful, it is even possible over time, he said, to transform an inexperienced young kid into a wise and caring president.

Sometimes he got tired of hearing me talk about my ambition, but he took me seriously. I appreciated that.

Out of the tote bag, Freddy took out two pairs of rubber gloves. We had taken them from the cabinet under my parent's kitchen sink. My mom wore them to wash the dishes because my dad said they kept her hands soft.

I didn't get why that made any difference to him, but my dad is weird that way.

And when it was my dad's turn to do the dishes, he wore them also. Mom said she liked his hands soft, too.

Freddy and I weren't concerned about keeping our hands soft, I can tell you that. The idea never even occurred to us. We were concerned about keeping our hands *safe*.

When you get right down to it, we were concerned mainly about keeping ourselves alive.

Each of us pulled on a pair of gloves. Then Freddy withdrew from the bag a small mayonnaise jar.

He had washed it twice and rinsed it thoroughly before we came. He said we didn't want the sample contaminated.

He unscrewed the cap and handed it to me.

He crept up to the edge of the water and

squatted down, putting one gloved hand on the ground to balance himself. With the other hand, he tipped the glass bottle on its side, dipped it into the lagoon, and filled it with water.

He stood up and extended the jar toward me. I screwed the cap on. Tight.

Rain pelted our faces. Lightning flashed so brightly that for a moment it lit the landscape bright as day. We felt like two thieves who had been stealing something from the middle of a major league baseball field when someone suddenly turned the floodlights on.

It fell dark again; the thunder boomed and echoed over the landscape. Freddy and I grabbed the tote bag and hightailed it for the edge of the compound.

I practically dived under the fence. Freddy shoved the tote bag through for me to grab, then dived under himself.

I held the flashlight while he filled in the hole in the ground. Rain slanted down hard, splashing our faces and washing the mud from our hands.

I grabbed the light and the bag, Freddy tucked the shovel under his arm, and we lit out for home as fast as we could go.

Chapter Eleven

The sign on the door said "J.C. Cumberton, Ph.D."

Inside, behind a desk where I would have expected a secretary, sat a young man with tortoise-shell glasses and neatly combed black hair. He looked like a model from a magazine ad.

"Uh, we're here to see Dr. Cumberton," I said.

"Fine," the man said. "I'm Dr. Cumberton's secretary. Please have a seat."

Then he disappeared into the inner office. I looked at Freddy and raised my eyebrows. *Secretary*, I was thinking. That doesn't look like any secretary I've ever seen. But Freddy seemed too preoccupied with our little project to even notice.

In a moment, the young man returned and smiled at us.

"It will be just a few minutes," he said, and started typing something on his computer.

Freddy and I sat quietly and waited. I felt

stuffed up and achy, and I was dog tired from having run around all night in the rain. Freddy had dark circles under his eyes, so I knew he was tired, too.

I leaned forward, propped my chin in my hand, and darn near fell asleep right there.

*   *   *

I had not gotten home from our little adventure at the milk factory until nearly 3 a.m. that morning.

I had opened the door as quietly as I could, turning the knob as slowly as a safecracker trying to determine the combination to a bank vault. I tiptoed up the stairs, peeled off my wet clothes, and, shivering, slipped between my sheets. I fell asleep as soon as my head hit the pillow.

It seemed as if I had been asleep for only about two seconds when my alarm went off.

I was in the middle of a dream about being out in the rain and the dark on the grounds of the Nacirema Dairy Production and Research Center. I thought the ringing of my alarm clock was some kind of security system going off, and I was about to be arrested or something.

But soon I realized that my situation was even worse than that. It was morning, I had gotten only four hours of sleep, and I had to go to school.

My nose was running, I felt achy all over, and the idea of falling right back to sleep seemed really, really appealing.

At breakfast, my mother heard me sniffle and asked if I was sick.

"You look terrible," she said, and felt my forehead.

For once, I actually tried to hide the fact that I was sick, even though it was a school day. Sometimes I try to pretend I'm sick so I don't have to go to school, but this was the first time I had ever pretended that I was well.

The thing was, I had to get to school to see Freddy and continue carrying out our plan.

"Mom!" I said angrily, batting her hand away from my forehead. "I'm fine!"

I staggered through school half-asleep. In geography class, the teacher called on me and asked me to name the capital of Texas.

"Nacirema," I said sleepily, and the whole class laughed at me.

After classes ended, Freddy and I held a conference. In other words, I asked him what the next part of our plan was.

He said he knew of a chemistry professor at

the local college, Dr. J.C. Cumberton, who could analyze the water sample for us and tell us what kind of poison it contained.

"Good idea," I said. "I approve."

A good leader always delegates responsibility, so I told Freddy it was his job to call Dr. Cumberton to arrange an appointment. When he got off the phone, he said it was all set, and we could walk over there that afternoon.

The college was only about a mile and a half away. Fortunately, the rain had stopped, but thick clouds loomed overhead and the sky looked dark and angry.

At the college, we had to ask directions about five times, and turn down about six different corridors, but finally we found Dr. Cumberton's office. And here we sat, falling asleep with our chins in our hands, with the mayonnaise jar of mysterious poison in the tote bag at our feet.

*   *   *

A buzzer went off on the desk of the young secretary-man, startling me out of my sleep.

The secretary picked up his phone. "Certainly, Dr. Cumberton," he said, and hung up.

"You can go in now," he said, and smiled. I guess secretaries are always supposed to smile, whether they're male or female.

I picked up the tote bag, looked at Freddy, and opened the door to the inner office. Together we walked in.

I had expected Dr. Cumberton, being a chemistry professor, to look like Albert Einstein. You know, an old guy with a gray walrus mustache hanging over his mouth and wild white hair sticking up all over the place.

Dr. Cumberton had gray hair, but it was neatly trimmed and combed. And she was a woman.

"Oh, my goodness," I muttered in spite of myself. "A woman professor with a man for a secretary. Weird."

Dr. Cumberton smiled.

"Perhaps *unusual* would be a better word," she said. "It may be a little unusual for a woman to make a career of science, more's the pity, but it does happen. You've heard of Marie Curie, haven't you?"

I felt my face flush with embarrassment. I hate it when I say the wrong thing.

"Yes," I mumbled. I cast a sidelong glance at Freddy, hoping I would not be quizzed on exactly who Marie Curie was. I remembered vaguely that she'd

45

been discussed in science class — but I never paid much attention in science class.

"And the young man who is working as my secretary," Dr. Cumberton continued, "is a student who needed a job. He's working his way through school and I was happy to help."

She walked behind her desk and sat down. Freddy and I sat in two chairs that faced her desk.

"Now," Dr. Cumberton said. "What can I do for you boys?"

Freddy started to say something, but I interrupted and talked over him. A leader has to do that sometimes.

"We have some poison we need analyzed," I said.

"Poison?" Dr. Cumberton asked.

"Poison," I said. "Very deadly poison."

Chapter Twelve

Freddy pulled the mayonnaise jar of poison water out of the tote bag and set it carefully on Dr. Cumberton's desk.

As we talked, all three of us stared not at each other, but at the jar of water. We looked at it in fear and fascination, almost as if it were not just an object sitting there, but something alive and mean and evil.

Taking turns, Freddy and I explained the whole story — how we had gone on a science class field trip to the Nacirema Dairy Production and Research Center, how I had looked out the window and seen the dead cow and the dying bird, how we had snuck onto the grounds of the factory and obtained a sample of water from the deadly lagoon.

All this Dr. Cumberton listened to with intense interest.

"I am very impressed," she said, when we had finished. "You saw a problem and wanted to analyze it scientifically to know precisely what the nature of the problem was. What an excellent plan!"

"Thank you," I said modestly.

It had been Freddy's plan entirely, of course. But I knew from my studies of the presidents that politicians often take credit for plans they had nothing to do with developing. They do it all the time.

One of the main jobs of being president, actually, is having smart advisors who come up with wonderful plans for which the president then takes credit. Freddy and I were a team, after all, and we had done the whole thing together. Maybe by now it really was *our* plan, after all.

Besides, one of the great things about Freddy was that he was just concerned with getting things done. He didn't care who took credit. So he wouldn't mind me implying that the plan had been mine.

Dr. Cumberton opened her desk draw and pulled out a pair of rubber gloves of her own. I liked that. It meant she took us seriously. I hate it when people dismiss what I'm saying and think I'm probably wrong just because I'm a kid.

She picked up the jar, taking great care not to drop it, and held it up to the light.

"Hmmm," she said. "Looks clear."

She unscrewed the top and held the jar under her nose.

"I don't smell anything," she said.

I started to get worried that she wasn't believing us after all.

"Really, I saw what I saw!" I exclaimed heatedly. "I know I'm just in seventh grade, but I do *not* make things up!"

"Easy, now," Dr. Cumberton said. "Just because a poison is colorless and odorless doesn't mean it's not there. To the contrary, it means the poison is that much more dangerous. There's no way to avoid it if you can't see it or smell it."

"Oh," I said. "Right. Of course."

Dr. Cumberton screwed the lid back on the jar and set it gently on her desk.

"I will do my best to find out what the nature of the poison is," she said. "But it may take quite a long time, and there are no guarantees I'll be successful."

"Dr. Cumberton," I said in a firm, leader-like way. "We feel this matter is extremely urgent. *Why* will it take a long time?"

The professor smiled kindly at me.

"You see," she said, "we have no computer into which we can just pour a sample of water and get a printout of whatever poison it may contain. We have to guess what the poison may be, and then test to see

49

if that poison is there. If that test proves negative —
that is to say, if that test proves that we were wrong in
our guess — we have to guess again and run another
test."

All this was starting to confuse me. I hate it
when scientists talk as if they're making sense and I
don't understand it.

"What do you think it might be?" I said. "Like,
I mean, what would be your first guess?"

"Most probably, it's some form of insecticide,"
she said. "Perhaps DDT or Malathion. If not, I suppose it could be some kind of rat poison, something
used to rid the area of squirrels or other pests. Cyanide, maybe, which can certainly be deadly, or arsenic."

DDT? Malathion? Cyanide? I wasn't getting
this at all, and I decided not to ask any more about it,
at least not for the moment.

"One other thing, Dr. Cumberton," I said. "We
did not have, exactly, you know, permission to be on
the grounds of the milk factory. If you could just, you
know . . ."

"Your secret is safe with me," Dr. Cumberton replied, smiling. "Actually, I'm quite honored you have chosen to include me in your little plan. I won't tell anyone else about it without your authorization. I'll call you as soon as I know anything at all."

Chapter Thirteen

For the next two weeks, time crawled.

Each hour seemed like a day. Each day seemed like a week. Each week seemed like a month.

Every time the phone rang, I was afraid it was going to be Dr. Cumberton telling me what kind of poison was in the lagoon. And then I was going to have to decide something — probably even *do* something.

If I found out that something in that lagoon was as deadly as it seemed, how could I stay quiet and do nothing? Lots more little birds might die.

And the lagoon was close to the river. What if the poison seeped through the soil and contaminated the Elkhorn? Who knew how many fish would die, and beavers and otters and even the deer that ambled shyly out of the forest and bent their heads to the river to drink?

Even if I wanted to ignore it, I knew that Freddy wouldn't allow that. His people, the Omaha, had been here before the white men. They had lived off the land and loved it too much to allow it to be poisoned, even by the science Freddy loved so much.

But I didn't want the responsibility of deciding how to solve the problem.

What was I going to do? I was just a kid! I couldn't save the world at my age!

And yet, I couldn't bear *not* knowing.

Maybe I had discovered some dark, amazing secret — something nobody else knew. I *had* to know what it was.

So I feared knowing, but I had to know. I didn't want the phone to ring, but I couldn't wait for it to ring. I was torn.

Time dragged. I couldn't concentrate on my classes or my homework. I started to feel really down and sad. I didn't have any energy. I slept a lot; it made time go faster.

It didn't help that the weather was gloomy, too. Every day was gray. Sometimes it rained, sometimes it poured, and sometimes the sky just looked dark and threatening.

I stopped off at Melvin's Barbershop on Main Street one afternoon after school, just to pass the time. All the old-timers there were talking about the weather.

Old Mel himself said he couldn't recall a spell of weather this wet since the great flood of 1927.

Then the rest of the old-timers started pointing at old stains on the sides of buildings and telling stories about water rising and cattle drowning and dogs howling on roofs.

That wasn't a particularly cheerful topic, so I headed for home.

It was a little windy outside and it was spitting rain. I walked hunched over, with my collar turned up and my hands in my pockets.

Halfway home, I ran into Freddy. We weren't hanging out together that much, because whenever we did, all either of us could think about was the lagoon and what Dr. Cumberton's tests might show.

"Hey, Melvin," Freddy said. "Any word?"

"Naw," I said. "Maybe she didn't really do any tests. She probably thought we were just pulling a prank. You know, I'm starting to think maybe I imagined the whole thing anyway."

Freddy looked at me with his dark, piercing eyes and said nothing.

"Yeah, you're right," I said. "I didn't imagine it, though I wish I had. I'll call you as soon as I hear anything."

We both assumed that Dr. Cumberton would

call me rather than him. I had done most of the talking, and she had looked at me the most when she answered.

I guess she recognized my natural leadership abilities.

But sometimes, I was starting to think, leadership just wasn't any fun at all. It was starting to feel like a burden.

I wondered how the heck had I gotten myself into this mess anyway.

I got home, gloomily shoved the door open, and shuffled inside with my head hanging down.

The phone was ringing.

I jerked my head up and dived onto the phone like a football player diving onto a fumble.

"Hello?" I said.

"Melvin?" a woman's voice said. "This is Dr. Cumberton."

"Yes?" I panted. "Have you found out what's in the water?"

"I have," she replied.

"Well?" I spluttered. "What is it?"

"I would rather not divulge that information over the telephone," Dr. Cumberton said. "Would it be possible for you to come to my office? This is something I would rather tell you in person."

Chapter Fourteen

The sky was dark and threatening as Freddy and I set off for the college. By the time we arrived it had started to rain.

I had called Freddy, of course, as soon as I had heard from Dr. Cumberton. He had met me outside my house for the walk to her office.

Now, as we approached the college, we both walked hunched forward, fighting our way through the driving rain. Raindrops stung our faces and ran off the ends of our noses.

Finally, we reached the building. We navigated our way up the stairs and down the corridors, leaving wet footprints on the floor, until we saw the sign on the office door: "J.C. Cumberton, Ph.D."

Soaked to the skin and looking none too calm, we opened the door. The male secretary sat there at his desk. His eyes widened a little at the sight of us, I think, but secretaries are trained not to show surprise.

"Go right in, please," he said. "Dr. Cumberton

is expecting you."

We looked like drowned rats, but Dr. Cumberton made no remark about our appearance. Actually, Dr. Cumberton looked none too calm herself.

"I'm glad you're here," she said, jumping up from behind her desk.

Her hair looked less neat than it had last time, and more unruly, as if she had been running her hands through it a lot. She looked more like Albert Einstein this time than she had the first time we met her.

Then I saw her eyes. A cold fear gripped my heart.

Her eyes looked a little wild and a little fearful — and not at all wise and calm and slightly amused, as they had before.

And if Dr. Cumberton felt a little fearful, then I felt downright terrified.

What could she possibly have found in our water sample that frightened her so much that I could see it in her eyes? What could have concerned her so much that she couldn't discuss it over the telephone?

"Boys," she said. "I think you'd better sit down."

Freddy and I sank into the two chairs facing her desk. But Dr. Cumberton did not sit down. She paced around her office, running her fingers through her hair and looking worried.

Freddy and I sat silent. And still Dr. Cumberton paced and wrung her hands.

Finally, she turned and faced us. She took a deep breath, as if she was trying to compose herself.

"I'm sorry it took me so long to find out what was in the sample you brought from the lagoon," she said.

Freddy and I said nothing.

"I tested for one thing after another," Dr. Cumberton continued. "First, I tested for DDT. The results were negative."

She paused.

"I tested for Malathion. Negative. I tested for cyanide. Negative. Arsenic? Negative."

She stopped pacing and looked at us, wringing her hands as though she was washing them in thin air.

"I tested for every kind of poison I could think of," she said. "Then I looked in reference works for rarer kinds of poison. And I tested to see if any of them were in the water. They were not. The results were all negative, negative, negative."

I cleared my throat, but still my voice came out in a squeak.

"But you told me that you had found out what was in the water," I said.

"I have," Dr. Cumberton said. "Finally, completely out of ideas, almost as a joke, I tested for one last thing. I was certain that this test would prove negative, as well. But, to my astonishment, the test was positive. I must say, my jaw dropped. I knew, though, what kind of poison was in that lagoon at the milk factory. I know now what killed the cow and the bird."

"Well?" I croaked. "What was it?"

Dr. Cumberton swallowed hard and looked at us.

"Anthrax," she said. "It was anthrax."

Chapter Fifteen

"Anthrax!" I yelled. "How in the world . . . ?"

I was shocked. I could not believe my ears. How in the name of Saint Peter could anthrax have gotten into a lagoon at a state-of-the-art milking factory?

I noticed that Freddy was looking at me with a funny expression on his face — sort of amazed, sort of amused.

"You know what anthrax is?" he asked. "I thought you weren't interested in science."

"Yes, I know what anthrax is," I said, still agitated by what I had just heard. "And this isn't science. It's politics."

Dr. Cumberton interrupted us.

"Sometimes," she said, "science and politics overlap. Why don't you tell us what you know, Melvin."

"Well, anthrax is a biological weapon," I said. "I guess you'd call it a germ that's really deadly, and some countries have developed it so they can threaten other countries with it. The way I get it, a little bit of anthrax can kill a lot of people really fast. If you released it in a big city, thousands of people would die."

"That's right," Dr. Cumberton said.

"I read about something that happened in Russia a long time ago, like in the 1970s, I think," I said. I squinted as I searched my mind, trying to remember. "It created a big political stink. I think there was an explosion at a factory making anthrax, and a lot people in the city that was right around there died. It's incredibly dangerous stuff."

"I am very impressed, Melvin," Dr. Cumberton said. "You are exactly right. The year was 1979 and the city was Sverdlovsk. As a result of the explosion, more than 1,000 people died."

"But here's what I don't get," I said. "The U.S. has agreed not to make biological weapons any more. So how in the world could a deadly poison like anthrax wind up in a lagoon outside the Nacirema Dairy Production and Research Center? It just doesn't make any sense!"

"I can answer that, Melvin," Freddy said. "You said it yourself: Anthrax is a germ. What it is really, in nature, is an animal disease. If you had paid any attention in science, you'd know that. Mrs. Ziggernaut told us about preventing outbreaks in animal herds, but you must have been daydreaming during that class."

I made a face at Freddy, but he ignored it,

"Anyway," he continued, "you find the anthrax disease in horses, sheep, goats — and cows. You said you saw a cow was lying right there by the lagoon. Obviously, that cow had anthrax and died from it right at the water's edge, polluting the whole pool of water."

"Oh," I said.

"No, Freddy, I'm afraid that's not it," Dr. Cumberton said. "It's an excellent theory, given what you know, but it is disproved by one scientific fact."

"What's that?" Freddy asked, looking perplexed.

"If the lagoon had been polluted by contact with the body of an infected animal," she said, "the levels of anthrax in the water would have been relatively low. Oh, the lagoon would still have been quite poisonous. Certainly poisonous enough to kill a bird. Poisonous enough to endanger a lot of people. I cannot tell you how glad I am that you boys were so careful when you collected the sample. But still, the concentration of anthrax in the water would be quite low."

"Yes?" Freddy said. "And?"

"The concentration of anthrax in the sample you brought me was very, very high. Unbelievably high."

I was thinking hard, trying to take it all in.

"None of it makes sense," I said for the second time. As I said it, I remembered vaguely having heard someone else use that phrase recently. But there was no time to think of that now. "So, how did the anthrax get there?" I asked. "Outside a *milk* factory?"

"I've been thinking about that," Dr. Cumberton said. "You seem to have read a lot about the explosion at the anthrax plant in Russia."

I nodded.

"Do you recall whether, after the explosion, the Russians admitted that the factory was manufacturing anthrax?" she asked.

I could feel the wheels of my brain turning.

"No . . . " I said slowly. "I think they denied it. But you don't mean . . . "

"I don't know what I mean," Dr. Cumberton said. "But right now, that's the only explanation I can think of."

"So that explanation about it being a state-of-the-art milk factory is just a cover story," I said, and a chill ran up my spine. "And what we have right here in Atkinson, Nebraska, is a factory that actually manufactures *anthrax*, a deadly biological weapon capable of killing thousands and thousands of people all at once."

Chapter Sixteen

Silence descended upon the room like a shroud.

This whole thing seemed too serious, too frightening, too deadly to speak of. I felt as if I were at a funeral.

For a minute, the three of us stared at each other. I felt very sad, somehow. It seemed impossible to believe that our peaceful little town was in such danger. To think that someone had put our town, and everyone who lived in it, in such danger on purpose made me feel like crying.

Afraid the tears would come and embarrass me, I looked away from Freddy and Dr. Cumberton and gazed out the window. Everything outside looked dark and gray and gloomy. Rain spattered against the window and ran down the glass.

I bit my lip.

Suddenly, Freddy, normally the most quiet of people, broke the silence with a shout.

"I knew it!" he yelled. "I knew it!"

Dr. Cumberton and I stared at him.

"You knew that plant made anthrax?" I asked.

"No," Freddy said. "But I knew something wasn't right. I told you — remember? The thick, heavy walls that you noticed, the heavy security, the fingerprinting, the people in space suits. Remember? I *told* you none of it made sense! None of it made any sense at all!"

Now that he said it, I did remember. I knew I'd heard someone say that before. And he was right. None of it did make any sense.

I realized that Freddy and Dr. Cumberton were looking at me, as if they expected me to say something. They were waiting for me to take the lead.

I knew I had to so something. Doing nothing was unacceptable.

I stared out the window, thinking and watching the raindrops streak down the glass.

"We have to act quickly," I said.

"Why quickly?" Dr. Cumberton said.

I pointed out the window. Freddy and Dr. Cumberton looked.

"It's raining," I said slowly, as the thought formed in my mind. "The river is rising. If the Elkhorn floods the lagoon or the factory, it will be polluted with anthrax. It will become a running river of death."

I paused. Neither Freddy nor Dr. Cumberton spoke.

"And the Elkhorn runs into . . . ?" I asked.

"The Platte," Freddy breathed.

"And the Platte runs into . . . ?"

"The Missouri," he said.

"And the Missouri runs into . . . ?"

"The Mississippi," he whispered. I saw horror in his eyes.

"And the Mississippi River provides the water supply for the whole middle of the country, from here on down to New Orleans and the Gulf of Mexico," I said. "I read about it once in a book on how Herbert Hoover got to be president. A huge part of the country relies on the Mississippi for water."

No one spoke.

"Dr. Cumberton?" I asked. "If the Elkhorn became polluted with anthrax in the concentration you found in our sample, and the anthrax was carried downstream into the Platte and the Missouri and the Mississippi, how many people depend on the Mississippi for their drinking water? How many people could be poisoned? How many people might die?"

"Millions," Dr. Cumberton said. "Millions."

Chapter Seventeen

The next few days were among the worst of my life.

Freddy and Dr. Cumberton and I decided that the only thing to do was to notify the authorities. The factory had to be shut down and steps had to be taken to make sure that the poison already there did not find its way into the river.

I started with the mayor of Atkinson, Mel Hootersen. He let me into his office, and listened while I explained the whole thing.

But he wasn't too happy about what I had to say. The whole time he listened, he looked as if someone were holding a piece of dog poop under his nose.

Finally, he interrupted me.

"Son," he said. "Do you know how hard I worked to get the Nacirema Dairy Production and Research Center to build its new factory here in Atkinson? Do you have the slightest idea how much that center pays this town each year in taxes so little twerps like you can go to a decent school with computers and all that newfangled nonsense? Do you?"

I shook my head.

"A lot!" Mayor Hootersen said. "Hundreds of thousands of dollars every year! And if that factory were shut down, do you know what would happen? I would have to raise taxes, and then I'd be voted right out of office. No one wants to pay higher taxes, whether it's for education or anything else, and they'd just kick me out."

"What about higher taxes so that millions of people don't get poisoned?" I said, a little angrily.

"Listen, son," the mayor said. "That plant doesn't produce poison. It makes *milk*, for cryin' out loud."

"But Dr. Cumberton told me . . . "

The mayor held up his hand to cut me off. He leaned forward and spoke to me in a confidential tone.

"Son, I don't care what that crazy professor told you. But between you and me, I think scientists are all a little nutty. I've never understood a word they said, and I'm not sure they understand what they're saying, either. Now, if you'll excuse me . . . "

He stood up and showed me out the door.

I tried to call the governor, but I only got through to an assistant. He said someone would call me back, but no one ever did.

I called both of Nebraska's senators and I got nowhere. On one of the calls, I heard the secretary cover the phone with her hand, giggle, and say to someone else, "This is so cute! It's some kid calling who thinks he's got a problem for the senator to solve."

That made me mad. I don't understand why people don't pay more attention to what kids have to say. They might learn something.

I finally decided that the only person who could help, the only person who could stop millions of people from dying, was the president of the United States.

I called information in Washington, D.C., and asked for the number for the White House. When I dialed, I got some man on the phone who said, "White House?" as if it were a question.

I told him I needed to speak to the president.

"I'm sorry, but the president does not take calls from members of the public," the man said in a voice as sweet and gooey as syrup. "If you tell me what you are calling about, your concern will be recorded and tabulated for our records."

"There's a milk factory in Atkinson, Nebraska, that's not really a milk factory but a biological weapons factory," I said. "And it's raining, and the river's rising, and if that stuff gets into the Elkhorn River it will flow into the Mississippi River and millions of people will die."

On the other end of the line, I heard the clicking of a computer keyboard. The man muttered as he typed: "Milk . . . weapons . . . flow into Mississippi . . . millions . . . die," he said. "OK, thank you very much for your comments, sir. I want you to know that the president appreciates your call very much."

Click. The line went dead.

I realized then that no one would help prevent this disaster from happening. Public officials didn't believe me, or else they didn't care.

The mayor was not going to act. Neither was the governor, and neither were our senators, and neither was the president.

If anything was going to be done to avoid this tragedy — if anything *could* be done — I had to be the one to do it.

At least I knew the score. It was all up to me.

Chapter Eighteen

Something happened to me in those few days. Something that changed me so much I didn't even feel like the same person.

I got angry. Really, really mad.

A disaster was bearing down on us, and nobody was going to do a darn thing. The mayor worried more about keeping taxes low than about doing the right thing, more about his silly little political career than about saving lives.

And the governor and the senators and the president of the United States all kept themselves so isolated from ordinary people that you couldn't get messages through to them even if the messages were incredibly important.

What good did it do to have those people in those jobs if they weren't going to do anything when it really counted?

White-hot anger burned inside my chest until I couldn't stand it. I was so mad I could hardly see. I slammed my fist into the wall of my room in frustration.

Then the anger drained away.

I saw clearly now that being angry did no good. Pounding my fist into the wall was about as much help as the mayor talking about low taxes, or some idiot at the White House telling me that the president appreciated my call.

Only action would help. But what could I do?

I sat on my bed and tried to think as carefully as I could. I felt willing at that point to do whatever I could, no matter how difficult.

My thoughts were interrupted by a noise in the outside in the distance. It sounded tinny and metallic, like a voice coming from inside a can of sardines, and I could hear it coming closer and closer. The noise blared louder and louder.

Finally, I realized it must be a loudspeaker mounted on top of a car or a van. As it came closer still, I was able at last to make out the words.

"Attention, please! Attention, please!" the voice said, echoing loudly through the street in front of my house. "The Elkhorn is rising. More rain is forecast. All able-bodied citizens are asked to report at once to the riverside to help fill sandbags and build dikes. Please, help save our town. The Elkhorn is rising. The Elkhorn is rising."

Chapter Nineteen

I met Freddy down by the riverside.

I had run down to the Elkhorn at once, of course. Building walls of sandbags to hold back the water didn't seem like a permanent solution to me. But if that was what was needed right now, I was willing to pitch in.

Besides, I couldn't think of anything better at the moment.

Hundreds of people had already arrived at the banks of the river, and more were coming every minute. One thing you could say for the people who lived around Atkinson: They would pull together and fight to save their town.

The river ran rough and angry between its banks, and much higher than usual. I could not believe the force of it. It looked powerful enough to uproot trees and tear down bridges.

And it was dangerously close to spilling over its banks and spreading over the flat lands beyond, flooding everything around — including the grounds of the Nacirema Dairy Production and Research Center, and, of course, the lagoon.

The area was buzzing with activity. Fire trucks pulled up, their lights flashing, and so did police cars.

In one area, one dump truck after another pulled up and poured out load after load of sand. People grabbed burlap bags and held them open while other people shoveled them full of sand. People heaved the full sandbags hand-to-hand-to-hand along a line of people that stretched from the mountain of sand the dump trucks had created all the way to the banks of the river.

There, people laid the sandbags one on top of another like bricks to build a big wall to hold the river within its banks.

I picked up a shovel and prepared to do my part. By helping to keep the river out of Atkinson, I thought, maybe I could help save the lives of countless people downstream.

But Freddy grabbed me by the arm and pulled me away.

"I need to see you," he said quietly.

He led me a short distance to a place where Dr. Cumberton waited.

"Let's go back to your house," Freddy said to me.

"What . . . ?" I tried to ask, but Freddy motioned me to be quiet.

In silence, the three of us walked until we came to my house. My parents were out, probably helping with the sandbagging. We walked up the stairs to my room.

Without a word, each of us took a seat — Dr. Cumberton at my desk, and Freddy and me on the edge of my bed. Freddy stared at me hard.

"Do you want to do something to fix this situation?" he asked me quietly.

"Of course I do!" I burst out.

"Why?" he asked.

"What do you mean *why*?" I exclaimed. "Because otherwise people will die! Lots of them!"

"And why do you want to stop them from dying?" Freddy asked. "So you can be famous? So you can be a hero? So you can get elected president?"

"No!" I shouted. "I don't care if no one ever knows who did what! I don't care about being famous or any of that. I don't even *want* to be president any more!"

"Then why?" Freddy asked.

"I want to save them for only one reason," I said. "I want to help because it is the right thing to do."

"Good," Freddy said. "Then I have a plan.

Chapter Twenty

It is almost impossible to describe what happened next.

Even when I look back on it, I can scarcely believe it. The events seem a blur. My recollections seem distorted. The whole thing seems unreal.

But I know it was real, because what happened afterwards was real — all too real, in fact, and deadly dangerous. And none of that would have happened had it not been for what happened in my bedroom that afternoon with Freddy and Dr. Cumberton.

"You have a plan?" I asked.

"Yes," Freddy said. "And you, Melvin, are the key to it all."

Me?" I asked.

"Let's sit on the floor, in a circle," Freddy said.

We did so, and Freddy held out one hand to me and the other to Dr. Cumberton. Then Dr. Cumberton and I joined hands, completing the circle.

"Do you remember what I have always said to

you?" Freddy asked softly. "I believe that we all have the power to change ourselves into whatever we want to be."

"Yes," I said quietly. A tingle ran from his hand to mine. "You have told me that many times."

"It is what my family believes," Freddy said. "It is what my father believes, what my grandfather believes, and what people in my family have believed for many generations."

Something in his voice filled me with calm and made me feel pure inside. I closed my eyes.

"It is not easy," Freddy said. "It takes work. It takes honesty. It requires a purpose that is clean and pure and not selfish — not related to fame or fortune or even your own personal happiness."

I sat with my eyes closed, letting his words wash over me.

"But it can be done."

I rocked forwards and backwards a little, listening. I felt Freddy holding one of my hands and Dr. Cumberton holding the other. It seemed to me that each of my hands began to tingle and feel warm and prickly.

"Melvin, I want you to listen to the words of my people," Freddy said. "You will not understand them because they are in my language, not yours. Still,

I hope they will find their way to your heart and do their work."

I cannot repeat the words he said then, nor can I describe the effect they had on me. They sounded soft, rhythmic, beautiful, and somehow filled with truth.

It seemed to me that I disappeared: There was no more Melvin, only truth, earth, nature, and reality. I felt the peace of the forest, the beauty of the animals, and the warmth of the sun, which makes all things grow.

I felt the happiness of babies and the wisdom of the old. I felt the joy of peace and the pain of war. I felt the kindness of justice and the cruelty of all the things in the world that cause hurt and are not fair.

Tears ran down my cheeks.

Still the rhythm and beauty of Freddy's words washed over me.

Then I felt as if I were being stretched in some grotesque and horrible way, like a doll made of bubble gum or a man made of clay. I could see nothing, but it seemed that first one arm was stretched to an impossible length and then the other.

I could no longer hear Freddy's voice. Surely I was flying through space. Everything was dark and empty. My legs stretched; my body warped and flattened and twisted.

I spun round and over, flying and floating. I tried to scream but I could make no sound. I opened my eyes but everything was dark. I tried to hold tighter to Freddy's hand and Dr. Cumberton's, but their hands were gone from mine.

I was alone.

My body twisted and flipped and rolled through emptiness. I felt scared and dizzy, stretched and distorted.

Suddenly, my feet touched something solid.

Everything was still black. My head was spinning. My hands pressed on something solid in front of me, propping me up. I stood for a minute, swaying, trying to catch my balance.

Then I heard the voice of a grown-up man quite close to me

"Mr. President," the voice said. "Are you all right?

Chapter Twenty-One

I opened my eyes and immediately closed them again. The light was so bright it blinded me.

Slowly, I opened my eyes again, first one and then the other. Light streamed in through doors made, from top to bottom, of small square panes of glass. Beyond, as I squinted against the light, I saw a beautifully landscaped garden, filled with bushes, trees, rolling lawns and red roses.

I looked down at my hands. They were braced against a carved wooden desk, huge and dark, with a surface about as big as my parents' dining room table. You could have set dinner for six on top of that thing.

I raised my eyes and looked around the room in which I found myself. Fancy chairs and couches were set in little arrangements around coffee tables. The floor was covered with a rug that featured, in the middle, an embroidered American eagle.

I looked up at the walls and noticed they were rounded, not straight. There were no corners in this room. The whole office was egg-shaped — sort of oval, actually.

Then I realized what had happened.

I was in the Oval Office, the office of the president of the United States of America. And I was standing *behind* the desk, not in front of it, so that could only mean, believe it or not, that I was now . . .

"Mr. President," the voice said again, "are you all right?"

I looked to my right and saw a distinguished-looking middle-aged man in a dark suit standing there, looking concerned.

"Uh, yes," I said, and my voice sounded impossibly rumbly and deep. "I'm fine."

Then I looked down at my feet and got dizzy all over again.

Not only were my feet in shoes that were polished to a shiny black gloss, but they had to be six feet away from my head! I had never seen them so far away. I felt like I was standing on stilts. Being a grown-up was going to take a little getting used to.

I swayed before catching my balance again.

"I'm fine," I repeated. "You can leave now."

"Yes, sir," the man said. "Remember, you have a cabinet meeting at 3:30, sir. Shall I come and get you when it's time?"

"Please do," I rumbled in my new bass voice. "That will be fine."

I was glad the man, whoever the heck he was, had offered to come and get me. Otherwise, I would have had no idea how to find the cabinet room.

He left, closing the door quietly on his way out. I sank into the leather chair behind me and stared around me, feeling frightened.

I was the president of the United States, supposedly a very powerful person. But I was all alone, and I had no idea in the world what I was supposed to do.

Chapter Twenty-Two

The cabinet met around the largest table I have ever seen.

It was large and oblong. If I thought the desk in the Oval Office was large, you could have set dinner for about fifty-eight people on this table.

I sat in the center of one the long sides. A bunch of grown-ups filed in and took the other seats as if they had been assigned to them, though I saw no nametags.

Most of the members of my cabinet seemed to be elderly white men. All of them sat down and put yellow, lined pads of paper on the table in front of them.

I guess they were ready to take notes in case I said anything worth remembering, or gave them a bunch of orders.

One man, a handsome middle-aged man with dark, olive-colored skin, straggled in late. As he rounded the table towards his chair, he bent his head close to my ear.

"Melvin . . . I mean, Mr. President. It's me, Freddy," he whispered, then headed for his seat.

Well, that was a relief. I wasn't quite as alone as I had thought.

The cabinet, I knew from all the reading I had done about the presidents, consisted of the heads of the main departments of government — the Department of State, which does all our negotiating with other countries; the Department of Defense, which does all our fighting with other countries; the Department of the Interior, which takes care of all the land the government owns inside the United States; and so forth.

I sat in my seat and looked around the table.

Every single person there was looking at me. No one spoke.

Then I realized that it was my job to run the meeting. And I did not have the faintest idea how to go about it.

I had to think fast.

"All right," I rumbled in my deep voice. "Let's do something a little different today. I want each of you to tell my your department's top priority — the most important thing you want to accomplish this year."

All of them looked as me as if I were crazy, but I had started so I had to go through with it.

"OK," I said, in a leader-like voice. "We'll start with ... "

I looked at the man sitting next to me. I had no idea what his name was or what department he ran.

"Uh, we'll start on my right," I said firmly.

I listened to one person after another. I realized pretty soon that the top priority of each person there was to get more money for his department.

The Department of Education wanted more computers, the anti-pollution people wanted more money to measure smog, the war-makers wanted more bombs, and so on.

One piggy-faced man in a military uniform made a big speech about how he needed more money to protect the president, namely me. He said that, with all the threats from terrorists in the modern world, the Army needed to help the Secret Service make sure the president was safe — and what the Army needed to do that was, you guessed it, more money.

"I know you want the very best protection money can buy," he said. Then he smiled a piggy little smile at me as if he had just said something very clever.

No one seemed to be saying, "My top priority is to do something good for the people of this country."

Until I came to Freddy.

"Mel- . . . er, Mr. President," he said. "Rather than tell you the Department of the Interior's top priority for the coming year, I would rather talk about our top priority for the coming *week*. And it is something that I think should be the priority of every person in this room."

"Fine, Fre- . . . er, Mr. Secretary," I said. "Please go ahead."

"It has come to my attention," Freddy said, his voice sounding deep and rumbly, too, "that in Atkinson, Nebraska, on the banks of the Elkhorn River, there is something that is supposed to be a state-of-the-art dairy factory. But I have evidence that, instead of milk, the factory produces anthrax."

Everyone in the room stared at Freddy. No one said a word.

"The Elkhorn River is rising, and more rain is forecast," Freddy continued. "If that factory floods and anthrax gets into the river, that poison could be carried downstream into the Platte River, the Missouri River, and on into the Mississippi River all the way down to New Orleans."

"Please go on," I said.

"The water supply for millions of Americans

would be poisoned," he said. "My top priority for this week is getting the plant closed down."

Out of the corner of my eye, I noticed that the piggy-faced man's face had gone white. His fat cheeks trembled and anger shone from his eyes.

"Close the Nacirema plant?" he shouted. "Over my dead body!"

Chapter Twenty-Three

The cabinet meeting erupted into a tumult of shouts. All those elderly white men began acting like little kids, yelling and pointing fingers and hurling insults.

I slammed my fist on the table.

"I will not tolerate that kind of childish behavior in here!" I boomed.

They fell silent.

"Now," I said, "I want everyone to listen closely. At our next meeting, I want each of you to present a new top priority for your departments — one that you choose not because it will get your department more money, but because it will do some good for the people of this country."

All of them scribbled notes on their pads.

"Number two," I said, "I want secretary of the Interior" — Freddy nodded at me — "and, uh, the general here . . . "

"General Burden," the piggy-faced military

man said, looking angrier than ever.

"Ah, yes, excuse me," I said. "And General Burden to meet me in my office in half an hour to discuss the Nacirema plant. Meeting dismissed."

All the cabinet members filed out, grumbling and looking at me strangely. As Freddy passed, I grabbed him by the arm and pulled him aside.

"Two questions," I whispered into his ear. "First, do you know who that guy is there in the dark suit?"

I motioned toward the man who had been with me in the Oval Office when I first morphed into the president of the United States.

"Yes," Freddy whispered back. "That's Mattingly, your chief of staff. He's your head assistant. If you tell him what needs to be done, I think he knows how to write up the orders and who to send them to."

"Second," I whispered, putting my lips close to Freddy's ear again, "and more important right at the moment. Have you managed to find the bathroom yet?"

Chapter Twenty-Four

I looked at my watch, waiting for the meeting to begin, and saw that I was wearing cufflinks with the presidential seal on them.

I wondered what I would do when it got to be time to go to bed. I wasn't sure I could get those things off. My hands might be stuck in my sleeves.

Then I began to wonder what other problems I would run into when my day was over. I would sleep in the White House living quarters, of course. But when I went there, would I find a wife?

Yikes! I don't like girls that much. I mean, a few of them are OK, but having one around full time? I don't think so.

Yet it seemed possible. Everyone around the White House knew *me*, even though I didn't know *them*. It appeared that I had not morphed into President Melvin, but into the president who was already in office.

That gave me chills. I must be President Clutter, I thought. Holy smokes, that guy was a jerk!

Now that was me? I was him?

I wanted to barf.

The door opened and Mattingly, my chief of staff, walked in. He was followed by Freddy and General Burden. I motioned for them to take seats opposite my huge, carved desk.

"General," I said, "what the heck did you mean that the Nacirema plant would only be closed over your dead body? Don't you see how dangerous this poison is to so many people?"

"Mr. President," the general began, and I could see that he was still mad, "you yourself approved this project. I see no need to go over it all again. You were thoroughly informed before you made your decision."

"Inform me again," I said. "I think Fre- . . . er, the secretary of the Interior has made some excellent points."

It was the only thing I could think of to say, of course. I couldn't remember the first time I'd been informed, because I hadn't been there, if you know what I mean.

"Well, the U.S. Army decided it needed the ability to make anthrax as a biological weapon," General Burden said.

I nearly jumped out of my chair.

"The U.S. Army?" I shouted. "You mean, that deadly poison is being made on the banks of the Elkhorn River by the government of the United States? What bonehead approved *that* idiotic idea?"

"You did, sir," the general snapped. His cheeks shook and spit flew out of his mouth as he talked.

"Well, I've changed my mind!" I yelled.

"Sir!" he yelled back at me. "The Iraqis have biological weapons! So, probably, do the Syrians! So, I'll bet you, do the Russians! Lots of our enemies have them. So we have to have them, too."

He was turning red. I answered him quietly this time.

"Do we think the Iraqi government is so wonderful?" I asked.

"Wonderful!" he sputtered. "They're awful! Terrible! Evil!"

"Then why," I asked, "would we decide that we want to copy their behavior? If they're so awful, why should we do exactly the same things they do? That doesn't make sense, now, does it, general?"

After I said that, I thought the general's head was going to explode. He swallowed hard and said that the Iraqis could kill millions of innocent people with their biological weapons.

"So we need to be able to kill millions of innocent people, too?" I asked. "I may have approved it before, but today I am ordering that the Nacirema Dairy Production and Research Center be closed, permanently."

For a moment, I thought that General Burden might cry. Instead, he stood up and marched out of the room.

On his way out the door, he looked back and said, "You'll never get away with this. Never!" Then he slammed the door.

Freddy, Mattingly and I were left in the room.

"Mattingly," I said, "see to it that the Nacirema plant is closed at once."

"Yes, sir," Mattingly replied. "I'm glad you've changed your decision, sir."

"One more thing," I said. "How did the factory get that name? It sounds like the name of some tribe of Native Americans, but it's not a tribe I've ever heard of."

Mattingly looked at me strangely.

"You gave it that name, sir," he said. "Because it's *our* factory, and it needed a code name."

"I gave it that name?"

"Yes, because it is run by the American government," Mattingly said. "Nacirema is American spelled backwards."

"Geez," I said. "That sounds like the kind of

code a kid would think up."

"That's what you said at the time, sir," Mattingly replied. "You said it was the perfect code, because adults never think like kids, so no adult in the world would ever figure it out."

"Hmmm," I said. "That was pretty good thinking."

Chapter Twenty-Five

I breathed a huge sigh of relief. The problem was solved. The plant would be closed.

I felt like exchanging high fives with Freddy and shouting "Wahoo!"

But it didn't seem as if that would be an appropriate thing for the president of the United States to do. Presidents tend to be pretty serious people.

Still, I felt pretty happy. Atkinson, Nebraska, was saved, not to mention the entire Mississippi Valley, down through the heart of the United States.

"Well," I said, sighing again, "I guess that's that."

The tension was gone. It was time to hold hands with Freddy, have him say the mystical words in his tribal language, morph back into myself, and go back home. I was so happy I almost laughed out loud.

"I'm afraid that's probably not the end of it," Mattingly said.

"It's not?" I asked.

"We have some work ahead of us, I'm afraid," he said. "It's not always so easy to get things done. There are powerful interests in government who want this factory to stay open. Maybe they're afraid they'll lose their jobs if it closes, because they're the ones who recommended opening it. Maybe they're afraid their departments will lose money. Maybe some of them really believe making poison weapons is necessary. But in cases like this, as you know, Mr. President, sometimes you can order something — and it never really seems to get done."

"Well, I want you, as my chief of staff, to see to it that it *gets* done," I said.

"There's another reason it's not all over with," Freddy broke in. "You can close the plant down, so no more poison is made. But what about all the anthrax the plant has already produced? Even if not another speck is made, we've got to find a way to stop the stuff that's already there from getting into the river."

"How can we do that?" I asked.

"I don't know," Freddy said. "But it has to be done in a way that is scientifically proven to be effective. Otherwise the danger will always be there."

"I wish I'd paid more attention in science," I muttered under my breath.

Just then, the phone on my desk rang. I nearly

jumped out of my skin.

"Hello?" I said.

"Mr. President, I have on the line a mayor from some little nowhere town in Nebraska," a woman's voice said. "He says he needs to talk to you, and he claims it's extremely urgent."

"Put him on," I said.

"Hello, Mr. President?" a voice hollered into my ear. "This here is Mel Hootersen, the mayor of Atkinson, Nebraska. We got a real problem out here!"

"What's that?" I asked.

"It's raining to beat the band out here!" the mayor yelled. He sounded a little panicked. "And I'm worried about that gosh-darned Nacirema plant. All your people from the Army told me nothing would ever happen, but we've had some reports of dead animals around that plant. I'm just dreadful scared of what's going to happen if the river floods that factory, sir!"

"How much time do you have before the river overflows its banks?"

"Hardly none, sir!" the mayor shouted, his voice quavering. "It looks like it's getting ready to flow out right now. And it's raining something fierce! Surely, it'll overflow that whole Nacirema field by the end of tomorrow. I'm positive it will. What are you going to do for us?"

Chapter Twenty-Six

I hung up and looked at Freddy.

"What am I going to do?" I said, almost to myself. "What the heck am I going to do? I don't know the first thing about science. I didn't think it would be necessary."

"If I may make a suggestion, sir?" Mattingly cut in. "I think this would be a good time to discuss the issue with your science advisor."

"Oh, yes," I said. "Good idea. Can you send for him, please, Mattingly?"

"Him, sir?"

"My science advisor."

"Of course, sir," Mattingly said, giving me a strange look. "Right away."

He left, and I considered the problem. Obviously, it had two parts: We had a short-term problem and a long-term problem.

The short-term problem was how to stop the river from flooding into the plant and carrying the anthrax downstream. The long-term problem was how to make the area safe forever.

They were different problems, undoubtedly with different solutions, but they both had to be considered at once.

The door to the Oval Office opened. Mattingly stepped in.

"Your science advisor, sir," he said.

Behind him walked a gray-haired woman in a dark suit and jacket.

"Dr. Cumberton!" I exclaimed.

Chapter Twenty-Seven

"I thought you'd never call for me," Dr. Cumberton said, bustling into the Oval Office.

"How was I supposed to know you were here?" I said.

"I was in your bedroom with you, holding hands, wasn't I?" she replied.

"*What*?" Mattingly asked.

"Never mind," I said. "It's kind of complicated. Besides, we have no time to lose."

Dr. Cumberton had been working on the problem. She recommended a two-step solution.

First, she said, we had to dig a huge ditch ten feet deep around the entire Nacirema compound and the surrounding fields. Then, she said, we needed to fill the ditch with concrete and sheets of plastic to stop the anthrax from oozing through the soil into the river.

After that, we needed to use a very careful process to take the factory apart and dig up all the dirt around it. All of it — the pieces of the building and the dirt from the field — would be moved to a special place where it could be decontaminated. All workers would wear space suits to protect themselves.

But both of those steps would take time — and time was exactly what we didn't have. The river was rising *now*. Within a day, water would flood the entire field, and the factory, too. Something needed to be done at once.

"Come on," I said, jumping out of my chair. "Let's go!"

"Where are we going?" Freddy asked, running after me.

"Atkinson, of course," I said.

"What are we going to do when we get there?" Freddy asked.

"We're going to personally supervise Operation Pots Xarhtna," I said.

The four of us — me, Freddy, Dr. Cumberton and Mattingly — barreled down the hallway. Mattingly pulled a cell phone out of his pocket and called the presidential security detail to arrange the helicopter trip to Andrews Air Force Base, where Air Force One was waiting.

"What the heck is Operation Pots Xarhtna?" Freddy asked, running along behind me. "It is named after some new scientific process or what?"

"I think," said Mattingly, snapping shut his cell phone, "it stands for Operation Stop Anthrax."

"You know, Mattingly," I said, "you catch on pretty fast, for a grown-up."

Chapter Twenty-Eight

We raced along a hall, through a door, and outside to the heli-pad.

But the presidential helicopter would not start. The pilot got all red in the face, but nothing he could do would make the engine turn over.

Mattingly whipped out his cell phone.

"Set up a presidential motorcade to Andrews Air Force Base *now*," he barked. "Tell Burden to organize a security detail pronto. The president's on the move!"

We ran back inside the White House, down a staircase, and out into a parking lot. The motorcade was waiting.

Freddy, Mattingly, Dr. Cumberton and I piled into a black limousine with little flags flying from the fenders. All around us, security men mounted motorcycles. With lights flashing and sirens screaming, we roared off through the streets of Washington.

We hadn't been in the car more than five minutes when the first shots were fired.

I thought they were firecrackers at first, but then the rear windshield shattered, showering us with glass. The car screeched to a stop.

"What the heck?" Mattingly shouted. "This thing is supposed to be bulletproof!"

All of us crouched low in the seat, out of sight, below the windows.

Gunshots exploded everywhere, bouncing off the streets, pinging against the sides of the limo.

"What in the world is security doing?" Mattingly yelled from the floor, where he was curled into a ball. "Why aren't they taking care of this?"

I rose up an inch or two and peeked out the back window. I saw no motorcycles, heard no sirens.

"They're gone!" I said.

We were alone, stopped in the middle of the street, with bullets bouncing off the car.

Someone must have seen me peeking out, because a hail of bullets hit the window, exploding it. Shards of glass fell over us like snowflakes.

"Why are we stopped?" Mattingly screamed. "Drive on, driver! *Move!*"

There was no reply. I stuck my head up just enough to peek into the driver's seat. The door was open; the seat was empty.

"He's gone, too!" I yelled, and another volley of bullets hit the car.

<u>Chapter Twenty-Nine</u>

Mattingly rolled on the floor, pulled his knees to his chest and began to cry. Bullets popped off the street and clanged off the car. Freddy and Dr. Cumberton hugged each other and sank to the floor.

For once, I felt mad at Freddy. It looked as if we were all going to die, and he certainly wasn't doing anything to help.

I felt like saying, "Got any scientific solutions for *this* problem?"

But I didn't. Saying something like that wouldn't help anything, either.

Another window shattered. I heard the sound of feet running towards the car. They were storming us now, I thought. No one was shooting back, so they were coming to get us.

Science could never solve this problem, I thought, but maybe leadership could.

Suddenly, I sprang up and hurled myself over the seat into the driver's position. I had never driven before, but I knew which one was the gas pedal.

I slammed it to the floor. The car rocketed ahead, tires squealing. We bounced off some parked cars and took out a stop sign, but I kept going.

The car whizzed down the street as I struggled to learn how to steer. The car careened down the street, swerving this way and that. Tourists on the grounds of the Washington Monument stopped and stared.

I yanked hard on the wheel. The car rose onto two tires and screeched around a corner. I straightened the wheel and the car raced down the street. Then I yanked the wheel in the other direction, and the car veered around a corner onto yet another street.

I was starting to get the hang of this.

Slowly, Freddy and the others rose up in the back seat.

"Hey, Melvin," Freddy said in a shaky voice. "There's no one following us. I think we lost them. If you could slow down just a little bit . . . ?"

"*Melvin*?" Mattingly said. "That's no Melvin. That's President Clutter."

"Whatever," Freddy said. "Can you tell us how to get to the air base?"

"Straight ahead," Mattingly said.

"Now, if only Air Force One will start," I said. "Or maybe someone has tampered with that, too, just like they tampered with the helicopter."

Chapter Thirty

Air Force One was the most magnificent airplane I had ever been in. It came equipped with a conference room, a dining room, a living room (with VCR, stereo, and a lot of telephones), and several bedrooms.

A butler with a towel hanging over his arm asked me if I needed anything to eat or drink.

I waved him away. I had problems to solve.

"I'm calling a meeting," I said, as Freddy, Dr. Cumberton, Mattingly and I settled into the living room and tried to catch our breath.

We had zoomed into the airport parking lot as darkness had been falling over Washington. After looking around for people with guns, and seeing none, we had sprinted aboard the plane.

Fortunately, the engines had roared to life right away. The people who were trying to kill me obviously hadn't thought I would make it this far.

Now, high in the night sky over Virginia, it

was time to decide exactly what to do.

"Mattingly," I said. "Have General Burden fired, please. At once."

"With pleasure," Mattingly said.

"Oh, and have him arrested, too," I added. "For being a traitor, and for trying to kill the president of the United States."

"Why do you think he did it?" Dr. Cumberton asked.

"He knew we were going to close down the Nacirema plant," I said. "And he obviously had a big interest in seeing to it that the plant stayed open. Whether someone was paying him to keep it open, or he just thought his job depended on it, I don't know. But he was in the process of taking over responsibility for protecting the president. When we headed for the airport — when we headed for Atkinson, actually — he decided he had to stop us. And he not only attacked us, but he ordered all our security people, including even my driver, to leave so no one would be protecting us."

"He obviously switched the limousine, too," Mattingly said, "for one without bulletproof glass."

"*Arrest* him?" Freddy said. "Let's just string him up!"

"Now, now," I said, smiling. "We don't do

114

things that way in this country. You ought to get your head out of those science books and read the Constitution. Even Burden is entitled to his day in court."

Mattingly was already on the phone taking care of it.

"Now," I said, "we need to figure out just what we're going to do when we get to Atkinson."

"Yes," Freddy said. "Exactly what is your plan for Operation Pots Xarhtna, anyway?"

"I don't know," I said. "I haven't made it up yet."

I asked Mattingly for a weather report from Nebraska.

He logged onto a computer and reported that the forecast was grim. It would rain hard for the next twenty-four hours, at least. Rivers across the state were expected to overflow their banks. Residents were being advised to abandon their homes and move to higher ground.

It seemed an impossible problem. How could we fight the weather? Against the forces of nature, we were powerless.

"Let me think," I said, holding up my hand to silence the others.

I felt terribly sad. Atkinson, my home, was in danger. I closed my eyes and thought of all the places

115

in Atkinson I knew and loved — the school, my home, the college, Melvin's Barbershop on Main Street.

I could picture in my mind the last time I had seen Atkinson. It seemed so long ago; could it be that it was only earlier today? Or was it yesterday? How did time work when you morphed?

But I could see it as if I were standing there still — all the people from the town coming down to the riverside to help fill sandbags and pass them hand-to-hand along a long line. And other people, working without complaint in the pouring rain, taking the sandbags and using them like bricks to build a levee, a wall, to keep the water out of the town as best they possibly could.

Suddenly, I opened my eyes and snapped my fingers.

"I've got it!" I said. "Mattingly, call out the Army!"

Chapter Thirty-One

All the next day, we worked through a torrential downpour.

The rain fell in sheets, slanting toward the earth, pounding the ground, stinging our eyes and soaking our clothes.

I pulled off my coat and tie and pitched in with everyone else. I even yanked off my cufflinks and rolled up my sleeves.

All around us, Army people worked with tons of heavy equipment — bulldozers, earth-movers, front-loaders, mechanical shovels and huge dump trucks — to build the biggest levee the world had ever seen.

The people of Atkinson had been doing the right thing, building a wall to raise the bank of the river higher and keep the water out of the town. But they couldn't do it by themselves. They didn't have enough manpower, and they didn't have enough equipment.

That was why I had called out the Army. Now, instead of poisoning people, the government of the United States was helping them.

All day long I worked, with my clothes plastered to my skin, shoveling, lifting, helping, directing people.

"I don't want anybody wandering anywhere near that lagoon!" I shouted. "Put up a fence! No one goes near there!"

A man in a military uniform walked up to me.

"Mr. President, sir, I'm General Wright."

I shook his hand.

"I want to apologize, sir, for the actions of General Burden and the others," he said. "Most people in the Army are good people, dedicated to helping this country."

"I know that, general," I said. "My grandfather fought in Vietnam, and I have great respect for the Army."

He gave me a strange look. I guess, as president, I was too old to have had a grandfather in Vietnam.

But General Wright let it pass. Maybe he decided he had heard me wrong.

"One more thing, sir," he said. "I can't tell you how inspiring it is to see the president of the United

118

States out here in the rain, pitching in like everyone else. It makes me very proud, sir. Very proud."

"Thank you, general," I said.

By late afternoon, the levee was finished. It loomed high above the river, and high above the Nacirema plant — a great wall, keeping the two apart.

Just as work ended and the last machine was turned off, the rain stopped. Off to the west, the clouds parted and I could see a patch of blue.

The worst was over. We would begin Dr. Cumberton's long-term decontamination plan tomorrow. Atkinson was safe, and so was the rest of the country.

Exhausted, I started to walk away. But people gathered around me and started clapping. News reporters stuck microphones in my face, and I realized that I ought to say something.

I climbed onto the back of a dump truck to make a quick speech. Below me, I saw a cluster of TV cameras and reporters. Then townspeople started to gather around, too, to hear what I had to say.

I cleared my throat, trying to think.

"I made a decision a couple of years ago to build a biological weapons factory here," I said. "That decision was wrong. I decided that the government would lie to its own people, and say that the factory produced milk when in fact it produced anthrax, which could kill millions of people. That decision, too, was wrong."

I looked at the sea of faces around me.

"Today, those decisions have been reversed," I said. "We cannot create peace by building weapons of war. We cannot save lives by designing things that kill. And we cannot keep democracy alive if government lies to the voters, the people who run the country."

I paused. No one said a word.

"But I want to tell you that I have never been prouder of this country than I am today," I continued. "People have come together to save their community and their country. The Army has been used not to take lives, but to save them. And your president has pitched in, just one set of hands among many, as all of us pulled together for the good of us all. And if I have been any help at all today, I want to say only this: Thank you, from the bottom of my heart, for giving me the opportunity to be your servant, a servant of the people."

Then I jumped down and walked away. Behind me, I could hear the crowd applauding, but I didn't care. None of that mattered. The only thing I cared about was that people were safe.

Chapter Thirty-Two

The next day, the papers were full of the news.
"PRESIDENT HAS CHANGE OF HEART," said one headline. "EXTRAORDINARY DAY IN ATKINSON."

Everyone seemed to think that President Clutter had done a wonderful thing and made a wonderful speech. Some experts said the president would probably be more popular now than ever, and because of that he would probably get elected to a second term as president.

I didn't care one way or the other. I was just happy to be a kid again.

Morphing back had not been anywhere near as scary as the first time. For one thing, I had known what was going to happen. For another thing, I had really wanted to go back to my own room and my own bed and the kid's life I used to have.

As I had walked away from the crowd, Freddy and Dr. Cumberton had walked up to me. We stood in a circle there in the field and held hands while Freddy said the ancient and mystical words.

The tumbling stretching, shrinking and warping through the darkness made me feel happy this time, not frightened.

Back in my room, Freddy had hugged me. "I'm so proud," he said quietly.

"Me, too," Dr. Cumberton said.

Then they left.

I looked around my room, happy to be there. But I took the poster of Mount Rushmore down off my wall. I didn't care a bit about having my face carved on a mountain any more.

When I grew up, I thought, I'd do something to really help people. Maybe I'd be a doctor, to help the sick and prevent disease. I could bring babies into the world, and give free medical care to people who couldn't afford it.

That would be helping people. But if I'm going to do that, I thought with a sigh, I am really going to have to start paying a lot more attention in science.

LOOK FOR OTHER

HUMANO MORPHS

DEEP TROUBLE AT DOLPHIN BAY

It looks like another bummer of a summer for Derrick Granger. His father, a marine researcher, is taking him on a field trip to a dolphin study site in the Florida Keys. Ten-year-old Derrick, a bookish boy who's fascinated by Greek mythology, doesn't even know how to swim.

But soon after they arrive at the center, Derrick overhears a conversation in which terrorists are plotting to kidnap the dolphins and use them to deliver nuclear explosives around the world unless they are paid billions of dollars. No one believes Derrick, and he feels powerless to stop the terrorists—until he stumbles across a strange seashell that gives him the power to transform into the Greek god Poseidon, ruler of the seas. Derrick has a fighting chance against the terrorists now—as long as he can steer clear of the family feuds on Mount Olympus.

LOOK FOR OTHER

HUMANO MORPHS

BLASTING INTO THE PAST

Something terrible is happening to Benjamin's family. At first it's almost too subtle to notice. His mother just doesn't look as attractive as usual and his father looks mean.

The situation gets worse. Family members get sicker and sicker. Terrified, they consult every doctor they can, but no one has any idea what is causing the mysterious illness.

The only way to save Benjamin's family is to go back in time and undo an evil deed done by a member of Benjamin's family many, many generations ago.

Benjamin and his friend morph into famous figures from the past. The boys go deeper and deeper into centuries long gone—becoming such renowned men as Abraham Lincoln and Ulysses Grant, Julius Caesar and Marc Antony—as they race against the clock to save Benjamin's family.